Baby, Sleepy Baby

Atinuke
Angela Brooksbank

For our Swedish Akinyemis with love. ~ **A.**

*For sleepy babies everywhere and to those
who love them so dearly.* ~ **A.B.**

WALKER BOOKS
AND SUBSIDIARIES
LONDON · BOSTON · SYDNEY · AUCKLAND

First published 2022 by Walker Books Ltd, 87 Vauxhall Walk, London SE11 5HJ.
Text © 2021 Atinuke ✿ Illustrations © 2021 Angela Brooksbank
The right of Atinuke and Angela Brooksbank to be identified as the author and illustrator respectively of this work
has been asserted by them in accordance with the Copyright, Designs and Patents Act 1988
This book has been typeset in Shinn ✿ Printed in China ✿ All rights reserved. No part of this book may be reproduced, transmitted or stored in an information
retrieval system in any form or by any means, graphic, electronic or mechanical, including photocopying, taping and recording, without prior written permission from
the publisher. ✿ British Library Cataloguing in Publication Data: a catalogue record for this book is available from the British Library
ISBN 978-1-4063-8957-9 ✿ www.walker.co.uk ✿ 10 9 8 7 6 5 4 3 2 1

Baby, sweet baby,

I'll call on the winds

and you'll sail like a ship
through the sky.

Baby, funny baby,
I'll gather the clouds

to cuddle you,
cosy and close.

Baby, happy baby,

I'll sing down the stars

till they dance
right into your room.

Baby, dear baby,

I'll beg of the moon
to smile on your sweet,
chubby face.

Baby, lovely baby,

I'll pull down the black sky

to wrap you in night's
soft blanket.

Baby, sleepy baby,
I'll hold you with love

as softly we drift
among dreams.